WILLIE MAYS

MLB MVP

ABBE L. STARR

LERNER PUBLICATIONS ◆ MINNEAPOLIS

SPORTS THRILLS *MEET* RESEARCH SKILLS

Lerner SPORTS

Free Database Trial: **lernersports.com**

Lerner Publications Company
An imprint of Lerner Publishing Group, Inc.
241 First Avenue North
Minneapolis, MN 55401 USA

For reading levels and more information, look up this title at www.lernerbooks.com.

Main body text set in Myriad Pro Semibold. Typeface provided by Adobe.

Editor: Lauren Foley

Library of Congress Cataloging-in-Publication Data

Names: Starr, Abbe L., author.
Title: Willie Mays: MLB MVP / Abbe L. Starr.
Other titles: Major League Baseball Most Valuable Player
Description: Minneapolis, MN : Lerner Publications, [2023] | Series: Epic Sports Bios (Lerner Sports) | Includes bibliographical references and index. | Audience: Ages 7–11 years | Audience: Grades 2–3 | Summary: "Major League Baseball superstar Willie Mays was one of the best batters and fielders ever. He won two MVP awards and the 1954 World Series. Discover more about his life on and off the diamond"— Provided by publisher.
Identifiers: LCCN 2022013937 (print) | LCCN 2022013938 (ebook) | ISBN 9781728476551 (Library Binding) | ISBN 9781728478593 (Paperback) | ISBN 9781728482668 (eBook)
Subjects: LCSH: Mays, Willie, 1931-—Juvenile literature. | African American baseball players—United States—Biography—Juvenile literature. | Baseball players—United States—Biography—Juvenile literature.
Classification: LCC GV865.M38 S73 2023 (print) | LCC GV865.M38 (ebook) | DDC 796.357092 [B]—dc23/eng/20220506

LC record available at https://lccn.loc.gov/2022013937
LC ebook record available at https://lccn.loc.gov/2022013938

Manufactured in the United States of America
1-52236-50676-6/27/2022

TABLE OF CONTENTS

THE CATCH 4

FACTS AT A GLANCE 5

LIKE FATHER, LIKE SON. 8

HEADED TO THE BIG LEAGUES 12

A LEGEND IN THE MAKING 16

HONORING A HERO 24

SIGNIFICANT STATS. 28

GLOSSARY 29

SOURCE NOTES 30

LEARN MORE. 31

INDEX. 32

THE CATCH

On September 29, during Game 1 of the 1954 World Series, the New York Giants faced the mighty Cleveland team. The score was tied 2–2 in the top of the eighth inning. Willie Mays stood in center field, ready to defend the Giants with his fast feet and rocket arm.

Willie Mays (*right*) chats with famous center fielder Tris Speaker during the 1954 World Series. Speaker used to play for the Cleveland team that the Giants faced in the series.

FACTS AT A GLANCE

Date of birth: May 6, 1931

Position: center fielder

League: Major League Baseball (MLB)

Professional highlights: earned NL Rookie of the Year in 1951; is a two-time MVP; won the World Series in 1954

Personal highlights: started the Say Hey Foundation; awarded the Presidential Medal of Freedom; wrote *24: Life Stories and Lessons from the Say Hey Kid*

Cleveland had runners on first and second. Don Liddle threw the pitch to Vic Wertz. *Smack!* The ball flew over Mays's head to deep center field. It would be difficult to stop Cleveland from scoring.

Mays sprinted to the center field wall and looked for the ball. With his back to home plate, he caught the ball over his shoulder while still running. Then he whipped the ball to second base. The runner on second made it to third, but the runner on first did not move.

Mays makes his legendary 1954 catch over his shoulder.

FINAL

SUNDAY NEWS

NEW YORK'S PICTURE NEWSPAPER®

10¢

Vol. 34. No. 23 New York 17, N.Y., Sunday, October 3, 1954

GIANTS CHAMPS

Crowd hails the conquering heroes as Giants arrived from Cleveland at LaGuardia Field last night.

The Giants World Series win was big news for sports fans.

The game stayed tied until the 10th inning when Mays got to first base on a walk and stole second. He made it home along with two other runners to win the game. With Mays's help, the Giants swept all four games of the series to become world champions. Baseball fans call his legendary catch one of the best plays in baseball history.

LIKE FATHER, LIKE SON

William (Willie) Howard Mays Jr. was born in Westfield, Alabama, on May 6, 1931. Many people didn't have jobs or money during the Depression of the 1930s. But Willie's father, William Howard Mays Sr., worked in a steel mill and later on trains. He also played baseball on a semipro team. Willie's mother, Annie Satterwhite, was also an athlete. She was a track star in high school.

Left to right: Mays, Giants coach Herman Franks, and Mays's father in 1964

Mays at the age of 13. He would soon start playing on his father's semipro baseball team.

Willie's parents were teenagers when they had him. They separated when Willie was young. Then Willie lived with his father and his aunts. Willie's aunts, Sarah and Ernestine, often took care of him. Willie's mother later married someone else and had 11 other children, giving Willie 11 half siblings.

When Willie was born in the 1930s, unfair laws enforced segregation. Segregation separated Black people and white people in places like schools, sports leagues, and restrooms. But Willie still played baseball with both Black and white children in his neighborhood. "We thought nothing of [playing together]," he later said. "It was the grownups who got upset."

His father taught Willie how to play baseball. Willie joined his father's semipro team around the age of 14. Willie could outhit and outrun the adult players. The team even paid him. Willie said that getting paid to play baseball was "like getting paid for eating ice cream." At 16, he joined the Birmingham Black Barons, a professional team in the Negro Leagues.

JACKIE ROBINSON

Baseball was a segregated sport for over 50 years until Jackie Robinson changed the game. In 1947, Robinson became the first Black baseball player to play in the major leagues since the 1800s. He joined the National Baseball Hall of Fame in 1962.

The 1951 Birmingham Black Barons

The New York Giants offered Willie a contract as soon as he graduated from high school in 1950. Eddie Montague, a Giants scout, said, "During batting and fielding practice, my eyes almost popped out of my head when I saw [Willie] swing the bat with great speed and power. . . . This was the greatest young ballplayer I had ever seen in my . . . scouting career."

HEADED TO THE BIG LEAGUES

Mays was 19 when he joined the Giants. But he didn't start in the major leagues. Instead, he joined the Trenton Giants, one of the New York Giants' minor-league teams. For the former Birmingham player, this was a step back. But he didn't quit.

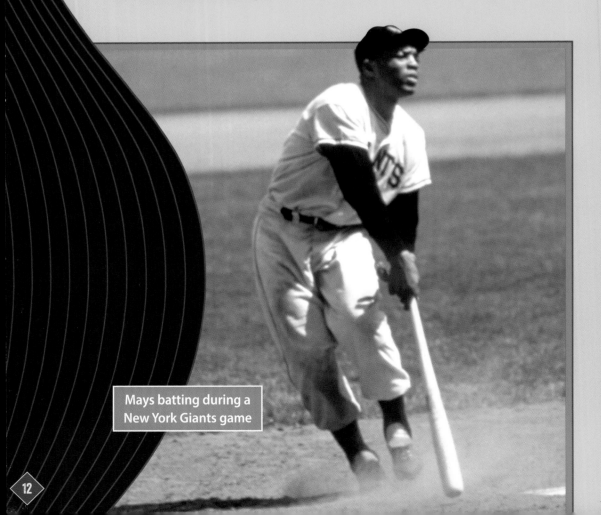

Mays batting during a New York Giants game

Mays caught baseballs, showed off his strong arm, and made over 100 hits in 1951. He quickly moved up to the highest-ranked minor-league team, the Minneapolis Millers.

Mays played well with the Millers. In 35 games, he belted eight home runs and batted .477. He made unbelievable catches in center field. In one game, a ball was about to fly out of his reach over the wall. But Mays dug his shoes into the wall. He half climbed and half ran up the wall to make the catch.

Mays made many incredible catches.

Mays (*center*) grins with Giants teammates Monte Irvin (*left*) and Hank Thompson (*right*).

THE SAY HEY KID

At the start of his career, Mays would often shout out, "Say, hey!" to talk to someone. People started to call him the Say Hey Kid. This nickname stayed with him for his entire baseball career. Mays also named the Say Hey Foundation using the nickname.

On May 25, 1951, while Mays was in a movie theater, the lights came on and a theater worker made an announcement: "If Willie Mays is [here], would he please report immediately to his manager at the hotel." Mays was nervous. He thought there was a family emergency. Instead, the New York Giants had called him up to play for their major-league team. Willie Mays was leaving the minor leagues behind for good.

A LEGEND IN THE MAKING

On his new team, Mays wore number 24. He started in center field and was third in the batting order. Mays struggled to hit in his first MLB games. His manager helped him adjust his swing. Mays smacked his first major-league hit on May 28, 1951. It was a deep home run.

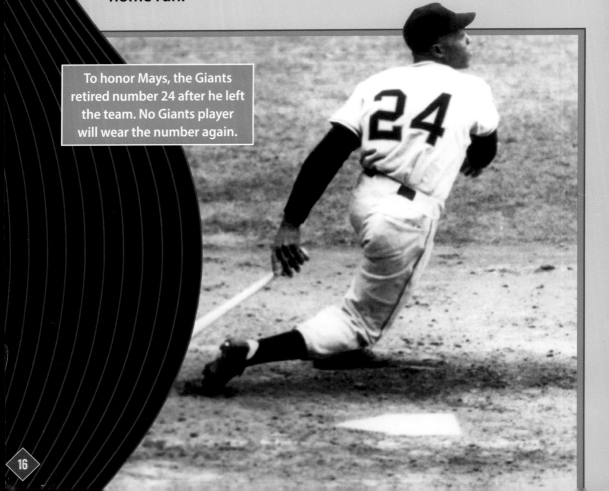

To honor Mays, the Giants retired number 24 after he left the team. No Giants player will wear the number again.

New York Yankees player Joe DiMaggio showing off his strong swing at the 1951 World Series

With Mays hitting home runs and making great catches, the Giants started winning more. Mays earned National League (NL) Rookie of the Year in 1951 with a batting average of .274 and 20 home runs. The Giants won the pennant and battled the New York Yankees in the 1951 World Series. The Giants lost. But it wasn't a total loss for Mays. He met his all-time hero at the game, Yankees center fielder Joe DiMaggio.

Willie Mays was ready to play more ball. Instead, he was drafted into the army in 1952 during the Korean War

Mays swaps his baseball shoes for army boots. But he'd still play baseball during his service.

(1950–1953). During his service, Mays trained soldiers to help them get stronger. They also played baseball together.

But Mays soon experienced great loss. In 1953, before his army service ended, Mays's mother died. Her death left him 11 half siblings to support. The next year, his Aunt Sarah died soon after he played in an All-Star Game. Mays went to Alabama to grieve with his family before he got back to baseball.

In 1954, Mays earned the NL batting title with an average of .345 and the NL MVP award. The Giants won the pennant, and Mays was off to his second World Series. In Game 1 against Cleveland, Mays performed his legendary catch and helped the Giants become the 1954 World Series Champions in a 4–0 sweep.

The Giants struggled the next eight years to win the pennant. But Mays kept smacking home runs and stealing bases. He had other wins too. In February 1956, Mays married Margherite Wendell Chapman.

LOSING HIS CAP

Mays ran so fast that he often lost his cap! Fans loved to see his cap fly off his head while Mays dashed to catch balls in the outfield. Mays later admitted he wore the wrong size so it would fly off easier and make his fans laugh.

Fewer people were attending Giants games. So the team moved to San Francisco for the 1958 season. The Mays family moved too. They also adopted a son, Michael, in 1959. But the marriage didn't last and the couple separated in 1962.

The pennant stayed out of reach until 1962 when the Giants tied with the Los Angeles Dodgers. In the last game of a three-game playoff, Mays hit the ball so hard that it blew the pitcher's glove off his hand when he tried to catch it! Mays also caught the final out. The Giants headed to the World Series to face the New York Yankees.

Mays with his son, Michael

Mays at bat during the 1962 World Series

The teams battled back and forth. But in Game 7, the Giants lost the 1962 World Series by one run. Even though the team lost the series, Mays ended the season with a league-leading 49 home runs. Mays had worked so hard without taking a break that he wound up in the hospital with exhaustion—extreme tiredness. While there, he rested to regain his strength. In 1963, he earned the All-Star MVP award. Then he won the NL MVP award again in 1965.

On May 4, 1966, Mays hit home run number 512. The fans broke out in cheers as Mays rounded the bases and reached the dugout. They kept cheering until Mays came out of the dugout and tipped his cap. He had broken the NL home run record. Four years later, on July 18, 1970, he made his 3,000th career hit. Mays was 39 years old and still playing strong.

Mays went through big changes in the early 1970s. He married Mae Allen in 1971, and the Giants traded him to the New York Mets in 1972. Giants fans and former teammates cheered for Mays even though he played against them. The Giants retired Mays's number, 24, that year. But heading

Mays smacks his 512th home run, breaking the NL record.

Mays watching one of his many home runs fly over the fence

into the 1973 season, Mays had sore knees and broken ribs. He decided to end his career after the season. The Mets played in the 1973 World Series against the Oakland Athletics. The Mets put up a strong fight. But the Athletics won the series.

HONORING A HERO

After retiring from baseball, Mays stayed busy. He joined the National Baseball Hall of Fame in 1979. In 2000, he started the Say Hey Foundation. It raises money to help children in need.

Mays smiles and waves to the crowd on the day he joined the Hall of Fame in 1979.

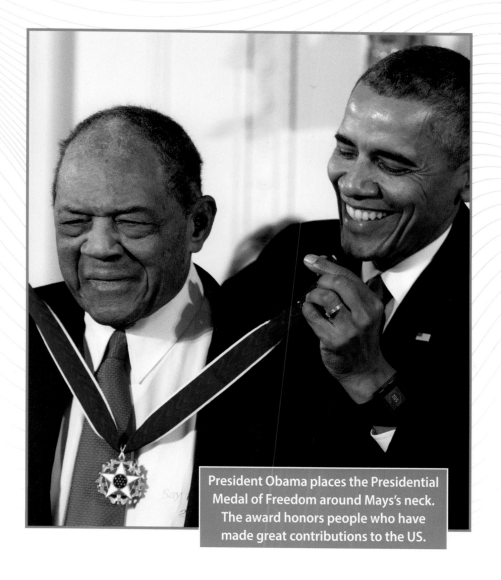

President Obama places the Presidential Medal of Freedom around Mays's neck. The award honors people who have made great contributions to the US.

Willie Mays inspires many. He was the childhood hero of former US presidents George W. Bush and Bill Clinton. And in 2015, then president Barack Obama awarded Mays with the Presidential Medal of Freedom.

Mays keeps his eyes on the pitch. Fans and baseball players are still inspired by his batting and fielding.

Mays continued to inspire others. He wrote a book that came out in 2020 called *24: Life Stories and Lessons from the Say Hey Kid*. In 2021, Mays announced that the television network HBO was making a documentary highlighting his life as one of the greatest baseball players of all time.

Mays enjoyed his life filled with baseball. He once said, "This country is made up of a great many things. You can grow up to be what you want. I chose baseball and I loved every minute of it."

Awards

NL Rookie of the Year	(1951)
NL MVP	(1954, 1965)
World Series champion	(1954)
NL batting title	(1954)

Career Totals

Batting average:	.301
Hits:	3,293
Home runs:	660
Runs batted in:	1,909
Stolen bases:	338

GLOSSARY

batting average: the number of official times at bat divided into the number of base hits

minor league: a pro baseball league that is not a major league

MVP: short for most valuable player

pennant: in baseball, a MLB championship where the winners go on to play in the World Series

playoff: a series of games played to decide a champion; in baseball, the playoff champions play in the World Series

scout: a person who judges the skills of athletes

semipro baseball: a level of baseball below the professional level where players are paid less than major-league players and don't play full time

steal: when a runner moves to the next base without the ball being hit

walk: a move to first base awarded to a player who during a turn at bat takes four pitches that are outside the strike zone

SOURCE NOTES

10 Allen Barra, *Mickey and Willie: Mantle and Mays, the Parallel Lives of Baseball's Golden Age* (New York: Crown Archetype, 2013), 39.

10 Donald Honig, *Mays, Mantle, Snider: A Celebration* (New York: Macmillan, 1987), 99.

11 Charles Einstein, *Willie's Time: Baseball's Golden Age* (Carbondale, IL: South Illinois University Press, 2004), 299.

15 James S. Hirsch, *Willie Mays: The Life, the Legend* (New York: Scribner, 2010), 77.

27 Joseph Durso, "Mays on the First Try, Elected to the Hall of Fame," *New York Times*, January 24, 1979, https://www.nytimes.com/1979 /01/24/archives/mays-on-first-try-elected-to-hall-of-fame-mays -is-elected-to-hall.html.

LEARN MORE

Britannica Kids: Willie Mays
https://kids.britannica.com/students/article/Willie-Mays/312401

Fishman, Jon M. *Inside the San Francisco Giants*. Minneapolis: Lerner Publications, 2022.

Lowe, Alexander. *G.O.A.T. Baseball Outfielders*. Minneapolis: Lerner Publications, 2022.

MLB Kids
https://www.mlb.com/fans/kids

Rogers, Amy B. *Positions in Baseball*. New York: PowerKids, 2023.

Willie Mays Facts for Kids
https://kids.kiddle.co/Willie_Mays

INDEX

All-Star Game, 18

All-Star MVP award, 21

Birmingham Black Barons, 10

DiMaggio, Joe, 17

Minneapolis Millers, 13

minor leagues, 12–13, 15

National Baseball Hall of Fame, 10, 24

Negro Leagues, 10, 12

New York Giants, 4, 7, 11–12, 15, 17, 19, 20

NL MVP award, 5, 19, 21

NL Rookie of the Year, 5, 17

Presidential Medal of Freedom, 5, 25

San Francisco Giants, 20–22

Say Hey Foundation, 5, 15, 24

24: Life Stories and Lessons from the Say Hey Kid, 5, 27

World Series, 4–5, 7, 17, 19, 20–21, 23

PHOTO ACKNOWLEDGMENTS

Image credits: Bettmann/Getty Images, pp. 4, 9, 14, 17, 18, 23; Andrey_Popov/Shutterstock, p. 5, 28; New York Daily News/Getty Images, pp. 6, 7; AP Photo, pp. 8, 22; Mark Rucker/Transcendental Graphics/Getty Images, p. 11; Hy Peskin Archive/Getty Images, p. 12; Charles Hoff/NY Daily News Archive/Getty Images, pp. 13, 20; Bruce Bennett Studios/Getty Images, p. 16; Herb Scharfman/Sports Imagery/Getty Images, p. 21; AP Photo/Rusty Kennedy, p. 24; AP Photo/Evan Vucci, p. 25; Diamond Images/Getty Images, p. 26.

Design elements: saicle/iStock/Getty Images.

Cover Image: AP Photo (top); AP Photo/TRB (bottom).